TOGETHER, APART

Together, Apart

second edition

Library of Congress Cataloging-in-Publication Data

Hoffman, Ben.
Together, Apart: stories / by Ben Hoffman
p. cm.
ISBN-13: 978-1-4951-7884-9

Acknowledgements:

"The Great Deschmutzing" originally appeared in *REAL: Regarding Arts & Letters* (2012).

"Next Time They Will Wow Them With The Shiny Stuff" originally appeared in *Treehouse* (2013).

"Your Baby's Mother" originally appeared in *River Styx* (2013).

"One For The Road" originally appeared in *Revolution House* (2013).

"Three And A Half Paths To Happiness" originally appeared in *Dogwood: A Journal of Poetry and Prose* (2013).

Design and Production:

Cover Art © 2014 by Nathan Pierce
Originally published by Origami Zoo Press

Published by
BULL CITY PRESS
1217 Odyssey Drive
Durham, NC 27713

www.BullCityPress.com

TOGETHER, APART

stories by

Ben Hoffman

BULL CITY PRESS

DURHAM, NORTH CAROLINA

TABLE OF CONTENTS

The Great Deschmutzing	3
Next Time They Will Wow Them With The Shiny Stuff	21
Your Baby's Mother	23
One For The Road	26
You Can Get Wet In Cooperstown	28
Three And A Half Paths To Happiness	30

The Great Deschmutzing

The first thing I want you to know is that none of us miss you. In life, Dad, you specialized in delusion (your own, mostly, but others' too), so I want to nip in the bud any notions of loss. You might have guessed I would feel this way, but what about the girls, do they miss their granddad? Not Marvel, not a chance—you know she has long been tapped into all that cruelty coursing through the Sternberg bloodline from you to me to her. But little Ellie would surprise you, even Ellie doesn't miss you. What seems like sadness is only that she has now for the first time seen death and is properly terrified. After your funeral, after we extricate ourselves from all your exes, Ellie starts crying in the car on the way to clean your junk out of the storage place, her head against the window, and Marvel rolls her eyes and teases, "Baby." I slap Marvel and tell Ellie that I am scared of death too, that it never goes away, but that at least this time it didn't get anyone we really care about. Next time, I tell her, we won't be so lucky.

Roy isn't in the car to stop me. Here is your I-told-you-so moment: Roy left me. The day you died—before we knew—I come out of the bathroom, and Roy is on the stool at the counter with a bulging book bag. I wonder: *did he pack that while I was in the bathroom?*

"I'm going to leave," he tells me. "Not for long. A few days is all."

"Do you want to talk about it?" I ask.

"No," he says.

Marvel walks through the room with her iPod in. She has turned part of her hair green.

"Why do you never want to talk?" I ask.

"Questions like that are why I'm leaving."

The girls will need dinner—Ellie, anyway; Marvel has caught not-eating from the other tenth grade girls—and I go get the chicken from the fridge and put it on the counter so it's one less thing I'll have to do later, after he leaves.

"Listen," Roy says. He puts his hand out to touch me, but he isn't sure what to do, and he can't take it back, so it hangs there between us. "It's like the X-Box game Ellie and I play, the one you hate."

"The one where you can hit someone after the play is over, and the ambulance comes on the field and carts them off while your player dances over them?"

"Yes," says Roy. "That one. You start out doing great, touchdowns, all that. And then, before you know it, you're losing, you're about to lose, and real quick before the game ends, you hit the reset button. Then you play it again, make sure you win."

Ellie looks up from some book. She is seven, and she knows this is a stupid metaphor.

"When I come back, we'll have a fresh start," Roy says. He stands up from the stool. He puts on the backpack like he is going off to school and will be home for his afternoon snack. His mouth hangs slack-jawed, like his arm before, like it has no concept of what comes next. I touch his lips, soft and pink, so different from the rest of his face, which is rough and acne-scarred. I want to remove them, like he is Mr. Potato Head, and keep them in my nightstand as hostages, until he comes back for them. He kisses Ellie on the forehead and whispers in her ear. He is a phenomenal kisser, when he wants to be.

• • •

Other than that, life goes on the same. I want so badly to be a good mother. But it is beyond me. Both girls are always dirty, always covered in something. Marvel: tattoos, piercings, eye shadow, zits. Ellie: mud, Crayola, stickers, ticks. They are almost as bad as your dog. Houdini is always dirty. He rolls in mud and he cleans himself in parking lot gas puddles. He has schmutz in the corners of his eyes, an inexhaustible supply, always dripping or crusting. And on top of all that there's the shitting-in-the-house problem. There is not much we can do about that. But the eyes we can work on. Ellie and I chase Houdini around the house, singing that it's deschmutzing time. We catch him and gently work our fingers through the corners of his ducts until they're clean. "*Vat* vee have *here* is a very elaborate des*chmutz*ing operation," Ellie tells Houdini. She says it just the way you used to. When the hell you taught it to her is beyond me. Sometimes for fun she sings it in the bath, while she is scrubbing her armpits or tiny toes. She can't get enough of it. Neither could you. Of course, she has the excuse of being seven.

Why did you get Houdini? For company, after Wife #4 opted to become Ex-Wife #4 and left like all the others? He was a puppy then, shitting all over the house and chewing your toes, which you could barely feel. Remember, once, when I dropped off some old-world tonic you believed would see you through another night, I tried to point out your age and the puppy's age. Tried to ask: Exactly how long do you plan to stay alive, Dad?

You didn't answer me but turned to your old friend, the light bulb in the kitchen of the house in which I grew up.

"*Vat* vee have *here*," you said to the light bulb, "is a daughter who *vants* her father to die."

"What you have here," I said, "is a daughter who got out of bed at one in the morning to bring her dad some herbal root shit. Drink up."

With regard to Houdini, the math, of course, did not work out in my favor: you made it six more years and accrued one more wife-turned-ex, and now I am at Ritz's Storage with my daughters and your dog, who is now, somehow, mine.

No dogs allowed, the attendant tells us when we stop by the office for the key. His nametag says Karl. He is just a kid grown old before he knows it, probably twenty-five, and tomorrow he'll realize he is no longer a teenager. He has a teenager's goatee, sparse and overly sculpted. I am about to explain that Houdini is your dog, and you gave him to me in your will, along with the job of cleaning out all your shit in storage, and that we can't leave him at home, or in the car, because whenever we turn our backs, he will shit everywhere.

But then Ellie explains, "Our granddad died."

"I'm so sorry," Karl says.

And then, because my Ellie is cute, or because Marvel winks at Karl, or because Karl imagines you went to school concerts and softball games and gave birthday presents, he hands me the key. He nods, as though we now share some deep understanding. I want to tell him that we do not.

The door to the storage unit has been closed so long it is almost rusted shut. Ellie chases Houdini down a hallway, laughing into darkness. Marvel abandons whichever soccer player she is sexting and helps Karl and me slide the door up. I almost expect secrets—you were gay, you had a second family, you were an ax murderer—but there are none here. Just things piled upon things, floor to ceiling. It is one of the horror movies you used to watch in the afternoon, surrounded by ketchupy wrappers and Slurpees and drawn down shades, only reversed: the living are coming for you, the dead, and you have barricaded all your furniture, all your belongings against the door to keep us out. The first thing is the piano. Mom's piano. Remember when we wanted to burn it in the pit in the backyard along with everything else of hers, only it was too heavy for just the two of us to move?

"This is going to take like forever," says Marvel. She examines your baseball glove.

"Do you guys need any help?" asks Karl.

"I bet you could help with the heavy stuff," says Marvel. "What do you bench?"

Houdini and Ellie reappear from the opposite direction they left and Ellie picks up the dog and puts him on the piano. She picks up the glove and puts it on her head. Clearly, she does not know where it has been—remember when I caught you with it? How unashamed you were, how you barely covered up? I take the glove off her head and announce the start of the trash pile.

"Something sad and off-key, Houdini," says Ellie.

"Don't shit on granddad's piano," says Marvel, and for once, Houdini complies with everyone's commands.

• • •

Speaking of shit:

Ex-Wife #4 comes to the door a few days after your funeral. I do not invite her in. Everything about her is unwieldy: her hair, her height, her bulky shoulders. She brings news: dog shit is not the only shit they found in your house. Houdini's is only upstairs, where you couldn't go after your second hip went out. "But your dad's," she says. "That's downstairs."

"His shit?" I ask. Ellie giggles milky Cheerios back into the bowl. Not Marvel: she eats no food, nothing to regurgitate. Besides, for her, this is an old word coming from my mouth. Are you surprised? Like father, like daughter.

"Yes," #4 says. "In the bathroom, mainly. Around the toilet. Some in the hallway." Suddenly, Houdini's affliction is making a lot more sense. Like owner, like dog. But I wonder, what kind of woman tells a daughter something so undignified about her dead dad? I think of all the times—around my friends, my boyfriends—you lacked the pride I wanted you to have, then how in the end you were too proud: too proud to tell your daughter you could not control your body, too proud to hire some help, too proud to go to assisted living. Or did I tell you not to, because I did not want to pay for it? Sometimes, Dad, I can't remember. Can you? I think of you, alone in that dirty house that was once so clean, unable to control your body, unable to go upstairs, unable to reach your light bulb, unable to bend and clean, and I am reminded of what Ex-Wife #3 said to me after your funeral.

As you may or may not know, Dad (does news reach you down, there, past the damp earth and lava?), numbers 2-4 attended.

Mom, #1, of course, could not, and the last, #5, stayed away, her wounds too fresh, I imagine. So: 3/5. Not a bad turnout. Congrats! Ex #2 and #4 sat next to each other, commiserating about what the man in the ground had put them through. About your religious peach-eating (for virility, you said), your monstrous farts, how you picked lint or dandruff off their coats in public, how you pretended to forget things when really you just didn't care. Marvel leaned over and whispered, "It's sort of like when all the victims' families get together to watch the execution." They were shunning #3, who had wrecked #2's marriage and then had hers wrecked by #4. If #5 had been there, #3 could have sat with her. But she sat alone, #3 did. Afterward, she motioned to #2 and #4, flinging dirt on your grave, and, indicting herself too, told me, "You gotta give it to him: he got around until he couldn't get around."

This is what I think of when I hear about your shit-filled house. You got around until you couldn't get around.

I tell Ex-Wife #4, still standing at the door with her giant blooming hair and American flag pin, to tell the cleaners to take all the time they need. I am not ready to go back in that house yet. I tell her I've been dealing with your shit, in one form or another, my whole life. She laughs and waits to be invited in. I close the door. Marvel goes to the window to look out at the woman she once called "Frankenstein" (didn't you tell her that was the doctor's name?—the monster is nameless).

"That's so weird," Ellie says, regarding your shit. "He loved having things clean!"

"Vat vee have *here*," I tell her, "is the triumph of a weak body over a compulsive mind."

Ellie does not understand. Her mind and body are both still beautiful, still pure, both growing in a perfect braid, like a magic beanstalk up into the future. At night, I dream that she is going to die. In my dreams, she is being stabbed to death. I am crying, and Ellie says to me, "It's okay, Mom, it doesn't hurt that much," but I can't stop crying. "You must be a really good mom," says Ellie, "since you are so sad." In my dreams, Marvel is nowhere to be found.

• • •

You always whispered to that light bulb in the kitchen; you wiped it tenderly with a damp rag. Your furry underarms, usually hidden, came out like deep-sea creatures when you reached to get its grime. You kept communion with it, told it secrets that you would not tell us. I asked mom why. "Kinship," she told me. "It's round and yellow and sweaty like him." At the dinner table, we made a game of this: How many ways were you like the light bulb?

Mom: "He's dim."

Me: "Too high and mighty for his good."

Mom: "Needs to be upgraded."

Me: "Easy to pull his chain."

You: "Good one, honey."

Mom: "Lurks over everything."

You: "Too hot to touch."

Mom: "Ought to hang from the ceiling."

Me: "Screwy."

Mom: "Doesn't do the dishes. Has never given me pleasure."

You: "That's unfair."

Mom: "To the light bulb, maybe."

You: "*Vat* vee have *here* are two very ungrateful *vomen*."

• • •

When Marvel is at school, I go to her room and read her diary. I can hear you now, Dad, defending me where others would condemn: *If you didn't* vant *me to read it, you* vould *have put it some*vere *I couldn't*. Her room is filthy. The floor is covered with thongs and ripped sweatshirts and drawings that both astonish and scare me: muscular bodies melting into flames, gleaming, sinister aliens, Japanese cartoons. When she was Ellie's age, she drew horses, horses, a thousand horses. *November 11: Jacked off Jim Kispaugh today. He came in like six seconds. He wanted to grab my boobs, ugh, probably would have cum even quicker if I had let him. Cum is disgusting. It got all over my jacket. Chloe said it will cum out. She would know. She also said Jim is a one-pump chump. Got a C+ on my science test.*

Yes, she is her mother's daughter all the way.

• • •

When Roy calls, I want to know from where. "Don't worry about where I am," he says. "How are you and the girls is the important thing."

"I'm worried about Marvel," I tell him.

"More hand jobs?" Roy always finds this amusing. An astonishing trick I despise but also want to learn, how he has mentally moved Marvel from daughter to some different category, so that her hand jobs can become funny, can serve as a shield. But, I admit, there is something benign about them, compared to the alternatives. I think she is still a virgin.

"I don't want her to turn out like me," I say.

"She will," says Roy. "She virtually already has."

"I don't want her to."

"I don't blame you," Roy says. Not cruel, just matter of fact.

"I want Ellie to be like me. I want Ellie to be the one who turns out like me."

"That's backwards," Roy says. "If Ellie were like you, she wouldn't be Ellie. You mean you wish *you* were like Ellie."

"Yes."

"Who's stopping you?"

I am in the near-dark, in the hall outside our bedroom, surrounded by photos of our family. We are at the beach, at Disney World, at a restaurant surrounded by nachos. Our smiles look lustrous, and I get close to one, like it is a mirror, and I try the same smile I have in the picture, try to see if my mouth can still remember the way. Please come back, I want to say. I will be someone different.

"What did you say to Ellie when you left?" I ask.

"On the couch? Just to be nice to you is all."

Somehow this is disappointing. I want something vicious to latch on to. We talk a little longer, about nothing. I am thinking about the day Mom left us. You remember, Dad. It was the day before they killed Martin Luther King. Mom squatted down for her big goodbye. She had caked on makeup, and her face was orange. You watched us from the kitchen doorway, where the light bulb could comfort you. The way you watched made me self-conscious; this was our moment, not yours. Mom hugged me. I wanted her to leave 1,000 times if each time she hugged me. I wanted you and Mom to be like Mr. and Mrs. Berkowitz: together, apart, together, apart. Lisa said her dad would buy her a gift every time he left, and then if she acted sad when he was gone, Mrs. Berkowitz would buy her something too. Whenever they reunited, they would all give hugs and go out for dinner and ice cream.

"Be a good girl," Mom told me, as if I had been being something else my first eleven years. "And don't take after your father," she said. "You don't want to end up sad and alone." (I know now, of course, that even in our final moment together, she was really speaking to you.) She held my chin loosely, like it was a cup of coffee gone cold, drawing it away from her lips, looking for a place to set it down. Outside her taxi honked. When she opened the door, the world was so full of wind I imagined she was jumping out of an airplane. I expected to be sucked out after her, to fall miles and miles into whatever strange place she was going to. But what place could have been stranger, really, than staying there with you?

• • •

When we watched the riots on television, I sat next to you on the sofa and made a giant pyramid of your beer cans. Once in awhile, you'd take a foot off my lap and topple the pyramid and I'd start over. All anyone cared about was MLK, you told me. Our pain had been usurped. But in my little brain, I pretended all the blacks were angry that Mom had left, that was why they were burning cars and breaking windows.

"This is the *vorld*," you said. "No one cares that vee lost our *vife*."

"She's not my wife," I said.

"The mouth on this one," you said to the light bulb. "The point remains the same," you said to me.

"I thought you don't love her," I said, for I had heard you say this many times, Dad.

"I do now," you said.

"That sounds backwards. You should have loved mom when she was here, and then not love her when she's gone."

"Oy, child." To the light bulb: "She tells me about love, this one. *Vat* vee have *here* is a know-it-all. Eleven years old and a regular love doctor, how do you like that?"

"I think she'll come back," I said, and what's awful is I actually did believe that.

"Do you?" you asked. I looked at you and—were you crying?

• • •

When Ellie is at soccer, I drag Marvel to Ritz's Storage. We sort through everything: divorce settlements, ancient Phillies shirts, letters from the IRS. "Trash," I say. "Trash." Marvel is always in favor of keeping. What does this mean? Sometimes she summons Karl and he helps us move the couch or the old kitchen table out back by the dumpsters. He has shaved his awful goatee, and in the Starbucks drive-thru, Marvel tells me this is because she asked him to.

"You asked him to? Why would you do that?"

"To see if he would."

"And how do you feel," I say, "to know that he changed his appearance for you?"

She smiles and looks past me, out the window at the menu. "And what do you think he expects in return?"

"My approval," says Marvel.

I look at her, intently, until her eyes go from the menu to me. "Mom, I'm not gonna like sleep with him or anything, Jesus. Get your coffee chilled."

That night, Ellie is being buried in cement. She is screaming. I wake up, Roy's awful breath on my neck, paw on my ass, but it's only Houdini again. I go to Marvel's room. She is not there. She has hung some of her drawings. There is one of us, her family, and it reminds me of the kind abused toddlers draw on television shows for the nice police psychiatrist. Marvel is ugly, Ellie like an angel, and then I realize they are flipped, Marvel is Ellie and Ellie Marvel. Roy is in a Red Roof Inn, in the top right corner, where the sun should be. You are underground, in a tomb, possibly with fangs. I am in my room, in bed, and my hair is made of snakes.

I go to Ellie's room. She still needs a nightlight; I want her to always need a nightlight if it means she'll always stay like this. Her finger moves across her face to wipe something invisible. Her face is perfect. But what I love most is that she is not yet old enough to understand who I am. I want to fossilize her. To freeze her seven-year-old's perception of me. I know her lack of understanding will not last much longer.

She is sweating. I roll her pajama legs up to her knees, and I open the window. Somewhere under those shimmering lights, Marvel is in the backseat of a car, giving (only, I pray) a hand job.

"Marvel," I whisper. "Please."

Ellie grumbles. The leaves rustle, either shushing my prayer, telling me to shut up and deal with it like everyone else, or maybe carrying it up to wherever it might be heard.

• • •

The next morning Marvel is back, and Houdini has something caught in his throat. He can't stop coughing; maybe he will die.

"You'd like that, wouldn't you?" says Marvel. Her eyeliner has crusted in the corners of her eyes and smeared her cheeks. I have the urge to wet my thumb and wipe her clean.

"We need to take him to the vet," Ellie says, and we do.

The vet's hair is different colors: gray, black, brown, and then I see it is not all hers, she has horse- and dog- and who-knows-what's-hair woven in to her own. There is a splatter of dried blood at the bottom of her coat.

"Whose is that?" asks Marvel.

"Can't tell," says the vet.

"What the hell?"

"Doctor-patient privilege," the vet says. She rubs Houdini's stomach. "Late night?" she asks Marvel.

"I'm sorry, do I look like an animal?" says Marvel. The vet smiles and says no, but I can see she *would* like to treat my daughter. After more rubbing, the vet coaxes from Houdini's throat a giant dust ball with a cigarette in the middle.

"Smoking causes cancer," Ellie tells Houdini.

The vet frowns at me, I frown at Marvel. Marvel exhales. "So he's going to live?" I ask.

"This dog is so healthy," the vet assures me. She pulls Houdini's jowls like a rubber band and lets go. "See. This dog is going to live forever."

• • •

Marvel and I are almost done clearing out your storage unit. The heavy stuff is gone, but Karl still checks in. He seems to be growing some mustache. Marvel tells me he is only twenty-two. I tell her she is only fifteen. She tells me she was out with him the other night. "Don't you even want to yell at me?" she asks. I don't, and she looks disappointed.

Afterward, at Starbucks we run into Ex-Wives #2 and #5. Strange, the way they congregate, like members of a cult or a book club. They are beautiful, specimens a hairy creature like you could never have won over. But back outside, with their skinny extra-shot lattes and their hair pulled back in buns, there is something barely perceptible that I cannot pin down, some slight deformity that might have allowed you to chew them up and spit them out. They are wearing scarves in the heat, and I think of the old tale where the girl tells her lover never to untie the ribbon around her neck, and when he does, off spills her head.

"You think your pop's in hell?" #5 asks me as we try to get away to the car.

"Given the way you did him in the settlement, I wouldn't worry too much one way or the other," #2 says to #5. "Hell hath no fury like a woman scorned, honey." She raises her coffee.

I tell them that I am a woman scorned, too, and that my pain is greater than theirs because I am blood and have first claim. I tell them: You only fucked him, and vice versa.

Their scarves constrict. Marvel grins and gives me her fist for a pound. We escape to the car.

"Ugh, I hate them," Marvel says. "Especially what's her name. I bet they're like lesbos with each other."

"I bet not," I tell her—though honestly it wouldn't surprise me. Any insights?

• • •

For two weeks after Mom left, you drank and slept on the couch. I didn't go to school, and the house grew filthy. Then the phone rang, and you answered it. You listened. You did not say a word, but then you did the dishes. The chronology is still murky—all our fights were circling this one, and we never quite got back to it—but I'm guessing this is when you learned that Mom died. Poor mom dead in the bathtub of some doctor's giant stone house in Germantown. You kept this from me for many months—all that time I wondered: why wouldn't she call? Why wouldn't she write? All that time you said: You know your mother. *Vat* vee have *here* is a mother who *vill* not see her daughter. And so I got excited, seeing your sleeves rolled up, those hairy arms submerged in the sink. I thought maybe we were getting back to normal: Mom had called to say she was coming home, and you wanted to clean the house. Then you told me to gather up everything of Mom's. We got her clothes, her silly romance novels. We put them in the pit in the backyard. We took photos from the wall and tossed them in the pile. Her needles and sewing kit, her spatulas and her blender, all her makeup (I hid a few lipsticks, saved them for one day, like maybe I knew). The Amish chairs she made you buy. You set it all on fire. You grabbed me by the hand, pulled me with you as you danced around the fire. (This is what I thought about, at every *hora* at every bar mitzvah—you and me dancing around mom's stuff while it burned.) It felt like we were witches, and later Mrs. Berkowitz called us Satanists. Maybe we were, or maybe it was just the flames, but you had me in a trance, dancing, spinning, and it wasn't until you finally got the hose and started spraying it all down—the fire, the pit, me, you—that I came out of it.

I asked you, "Daddy, what are we doing exactly?"

You swept your hand across the lawn. "*Vat* vee have *here*," you said—but then you did not finish. Instead, you kept spraying until the fire was out, and Mom's stuff was half-ashes, and we were soaking wet.

• • •

I cannot find the girls. Marvel has taken Ellie. I want to feel panic, but I don't have it in me right now. So I go to Marvel's room and read her diary.

August 22: My mom is such a bitch. But then so am I.

Reading this I feel a connection with her, like we finally know each other.

January 19: Dad left. I hate him, but at the same time, I don't blame him.

I promise myself I will never read Ellie's diary, when she keeps one. What do you think, Dad, are the odds of me keeping that promise? *Vat* vee have *here* is a mother who *vill* not *vee* able to keep her *vord*. I go downstairs and watch the news, which always brings me comfort. Fathers are touching their daughters, mothers are putting their babies in freezers, and I tell myself: I am an awful mother, I do terrible things to my children—and yet! I am not those other people. I never could be. There is a line that they have crossed, and even if I wanted to, the line is hidden so far away inside that I would not even know where or how to find it.

When the girls finally come home, the sky outside is a dark purple. "Just like I told you to," Marvel says to Ellie, and Ellie runs to me and says, "Look, Mom, look what I got!" Her shirt is knotted to her midriff—Marvel has taught her this; I taught Marvel, back when she and I were both so much younger. Ellie turns her back to me, and she is wild with laughter, in awe of everything. She has a tattoo of an elephant across her lower back.

"Marvel took me to get a tramp stamp!" Ellie says.

Marvel grins. "She'll be the coolest girl in the whole second grade."

"That better freaking just be henna," I tell Ellie. "You won't be able to be buried in the cemetery with us. You'll be with Marvel in the cemetery for bad daughters who get tattoos. You think you're scared of death now, wait until you can't be dead with the rest of your family."

"I don't care about my family," Ellie says.

I slap her, right across her mouth and cheek. Even Marvel gasps. Ellie's lip trembles, then her whole body.

"I didn't tell her to say that," Marvel says. In the way her shoulders rise, I can see her triumph: *at last the little brat gets it.* But then she puts her arm around Ellie and tells her it will be okay; she is a veteran when it comes to this. She will teach Ellie how she can use this sort of thing against me, how to slap the spot I slapped so it will look slapped for longer.

I go to the bathroom and lock myself there. All evening I lie beneath the toilet, nose pressed to the porcelain, crying, pulling my hair as hard as I can, until some comes out in clumps. I can hear the girls laughing and playing. I hear Marvel explaining, "You never put a friend who's hotter than you in your profile picture."

When I finally emerge, only Houdini cares. The house is quiet. He licks my tears, presents his eyes for deschmutzing, then he starts to shit, and I don't even have it in me to drag him outside.

The phone rings. It is Roy, and this time when I ask where he is, he doesn't say, "Don't worry where I am."

I drive to the motel, and when Roy opens the door, we skip speaking and go straight to biting. Roy is throwing me around the bed, tugging, twisting, and slapping, grinding my face into the pillow, and then he slows down.

"What happened to your hair?" he says.

"Nothing," I say. "Hey. Come on."

"What do you mean nothing? It looks like some of it's pulled out here," he says.

"You were pulling too hard," I say.

"What? No, I wasn't. Was I? Jesus, why didn't you tell me to stop?"

"Don't stop," I say, but he already has. He flops down next to me and strokes my back. It feels like he is drawing something in particular. I am still on my hands and knees, and I stay like that for a few seconds before I roll over.

He has all his socks and boxers and T-shirts stacked on top of the dresser, which gives me some sort of silly hope.

"Well," he says. "Just like old times."

I am trying to remember the last time Roy and I shared a hotel room and if he stacked his clothes on the dresser or in the dresser or kept them in suitcase or what.

He pokes me. "That was a joke."

The last time we shared a hotel was Mexico. Remember, when Marvel was seven and starting to exhibit signs of becoming like you and me, we paid you (thanks, Dad) to take her for a week so we could ride a tiny plane that shoved Roy and I too close together for too long and then almost blew apart halfway there. Taxco was a white-walled city on the side of a mountain, from which they drew silver. We ate at a restaurant where the waiter returned to the table and regretted to inform us they were out of pasta. What about bread, I said, are you out of bread? Bread we have, the waiter told us. After dinner, we fucked gently for a change; we knew about Ellie. I didn't want another baby, but I'd have babies if it meant gentle sex. Roy cupped my breasts instead of twisting. We nuzzled naked on our balcony. I lay back against Roy and felt the air go out of his chest. His hair tickled my back. He held his beer against my neck. The stars were low, hovering just over the mountain, which was darker than the sky. From my angle, the entire world was on a slope. It seemed we would slide off the balcony. Roy grasped my belly with his fingers, found Ellie, named her, molded her to be the way he wanted.

• • •

When I get dressed, Roy is half-asleep.

"Do you want me to turn on Sportscenter, or will you be okay?"

He gives me a thumbs up.

When I get home, there is a car in the driveway with a bumper sticker that reads, "Melt Hearts Not Planets." I know it is Karl from storage, and I can barely stop myself from accelerating into it. When I go inside, Karl is right in front of me in the laundry room holding my underwear. But he is only folding clothes that have been sitting some time in the basket. He won't look at me. Marvel and Ellie are sitting on the steps cleaning Houdini's eyes. Marvel's hair is not green, it is brown again—when did this happen? Her forehead holds a constellation of pimples. She seems so tiny, like she is shriveling up in front of me.

She holds up a hand, full of my hair. She asks, "Mom, did you do this because of me?"

"Oh, cutie," I say. I want to say more—this is when I should throw Karl out of my house, defend her little body for her—but I can't, I am crying, and Marvel does not know what to say or do. I want so badly to give her a hug, but she says, "Sorry," and she runs up to her room, my hair drifting down the stairs behind her. Karl looks up from some socks, and when he does, I see how clean-shaven his face his. Without the hair, I can see so clearly every way he feels about her.

Little Ellie leaves Houdini, and she walks past me into the dark kitchen. She is wearing one of Marvel's sweatshirts, torn from the neck. I follow her, crying, and when she opens the fridge, I can see in the light her cheek, red and bruised.

"Cutie," I say—this is all I can do tonight, say "cutie" and cry.

She gets a juice box from the fridge and she looks at me, she sees me exactly. "Cutie?"

She leaves the kitchen as Karl comes in and pats her on her little head. They have made mac and cheese, which is on the counter, and Karl scoops it into two bowls. He puts one bowl in front of me, and then he takes the other upstairs to Marvel to feed her and fuck her and comfort her.

I decide I will go upstairs in a few minutes, once I am organized. First, I get the magnetized notepad Roy and I used to make grocery lists on, and I sit on the kitchen counter in the dark. I turn the pad sideways and make five columns, one for each of us, and I start to make a list of the things I need to get rid of, to throw out or burn or zap or scrub away, so that when I'm done my daughters and I won't recognize each other. We will meet, sort of like strangers, and they won't even know who I was.

<u>Roy</u>	<u>Marvel</u>	<u>Dad</u>	<u>Ellie</u>	<u>Me</u>
clothes tools toiletries DVDs video games our photos our videos (everything)	diary slutty clothes piercings tattoos Karl not eating	everything left in storage exes probably Houdini?	henna tattoo slap mark facebook account?	

My list should probably be the longest, but I don't know where to start.

Next Time They Will Wow Them With The Shiny Stuff

Luckily, the Indians see them coming. They see the sails. They are picnicking, the Indians. They have spread their blankets up on the rocks, where there is a sea breeze that goes well with their Pinot Blanc. From up there, they see the sails, and then the ships bouncing in the waves.

So: they put away the good stuff. They hide their iPods. They haul their TVs up trees, bind them to the highest branches. They bury their DVD collections deep in the dirt. They sink their SUVs in the lake (they have to roll up their sleeves, lean out of their canoes, and hold the vehicles down until they stay down). They eat all the junk food, gorge themselves on fruit snacks and chocolate chip cookies until they feel they will burst and their chins are stained (wild berry juice, they will tell the strangers). They burn all the receipts. They disguise their lawnmowers as deer. They send their most beautiful women west. Don't ever turn back, they tell them. Take the X-boxes. Take the Xanax.

When the strangers land, when they come sick and tired off the ships, the Indians offer them their very best: gourds, pumpkins, spoiled corn. The strangers have no manners. They could use some sunscreen. They could use some floss. Their belt buckles remind the Indians of their fine silverware, packed safely away.

What are you about? the strangers ask. They point and wave their arms in giant circles so the Indians will understand. The Indians tell them (tell them with straight faces, no less—only a few children giggle: what a great joke this is!) that they worship the sun and the moon. Also the rain and the trees. The wolf. The earth, which glistens, as if packed with jewels.

Your Baby's Mother

I. Conception, Sort Of

Junior year, you and Mora have a baby together. When Mr. Renola draws her name with yours from the bin, Innis winks at you: Mora has a reputation. You go up to the front of the class to get your baby, and Mr. Renola asks, "Boy or girl?" Instantly you get how stupid this is: it's not like in real life you'll get to choose.

"Boy," you say.

"Girl," says Mora.

"Off to a great start," says Innis.

"I'm the man," you shout, because the guys are watching. "I pay the bills, don't I?"

"Honey," says Mora, because the girls are watching, too. "You don't want to be so stubborn before we've even consummated our relationship, do you?"

"Consummated?" says Innis. "You got a baby!"

"Adopted," says Mora, reaching past the blue eggs for a pink one.

II. Infancy

So you and Mora take turns carrying around your baby girl. In public school, they get real eggs because any day now they'll be having real babies, but at academy, you get plastic, which lowers the stakes. You cradle your baby in your lacrosse stick and toss her off lockers. Mora hides contraband gum in the egg and keeps the egg in her bra. You are jealous of your baby. You also worry that many guys will have opportunity to steal her.

But it's you who loses the baby. You leave her on your desk in history, and when you come back from the bathroom, she's gone. You look all over. You're in the middle of a unit on the Industrial Revolution, but Mr. Saffo is talking about the Lindbergh kidnapping. Finally he makes some joke about the Eggmancipation Proclamation, and you get wise.

"Can I please have my baby back?"

Teachers always want to teach you, and Mr. Saffo says, "Do you see a lesson here?"

No, you don't.

Mr. Saffo says, "Never leave your baby with someone you don't trust."

"I didn't! I left her with a teacher!"

"The lesson," says Innis, "is don't trust your teachers."

III. Adolescence

Still, you could've paid Mr. Saffo's ransom. You live so much better than the other couples struggling at McDonald's because Mora gets a job stripping. Mr. Renola is pissed, but Mora played by the rules: she found the job in the local classifieds; she has the requisite level of education. She works five nights a week, 2,000 bucks a night (or so the ad claims). You find a house with a pool in a good district, and you don't even need to work. Turns out you *don't* pay the bills.

Innis says, "Feminism."

Mr. Renola says, "Innis, *stop* talking."

You show Mr. Renola your spreadsheet; the numbers add up. All he can do is give you an A and clarify the guidelines for next year's parents: no stripping to support the baby and the father must get a job.

IV. Adulthood, Or Something

So of course the next year at graduation, Mora is pregnant. She is the only one for whom no college plans are announced—Innis' folks pulled strings at State—and you wonder if she held on to that classified ad. During the valedictory, you and Innis try to guess the dad, though probably he is from public school. Innis jokes that you paved the way, but you both know other guys paved it long before you never did. Her stomach swells under her robe. You get a little hard, and you feel a little bad at the same time, like maybe somehow you *were* the one to start it all. Remember how you never let her name it, how when she proposed Ella or Sarah-Lynn, you came back with Over-Easy or Cadbury. Remember you caught her under the art stairwell. No, not when she was topless with Brian McInnity. The other time. From the doorway, she looked flushed. Humming to the egg, pressing it to her cheek.

One For The Road

Mom and Dad watch the apocalypse on TV. Correction: they watch Cronkite talking about the apocalypse on TV. But let's not split hairs. Like usual, Dad waited 'til the last second and all the good motels were booked, so they stay at a brothel in the hills, where the air is sticky. Bed is too, come to mention it. Mom blows bubbles with a plastic wand, strokes her swollen belly. Dad takes notes in this joint's Bible, a *Hustler* from the bedside dresser. Dad says Mom's bubbles look like mushroom clouds.

Mom says this is only priming effect.

Dad says: Psychobabble, always with the psychobabble. End of the world and still the psychobabble!

This is Pennsylvania, this is 1979, this is time for a pact: If they live, they will name you Earnest. If not, Charlie.

Moans that sound, well, let's say practiced if not perfected, come through the walls and mingle with Cronkite babbling on the crackling Zenith: *Ooh Roger the worst accident of the nuclear age ooh Roger the danger tonight is that it could get much worse ooh Roger you made the damn leap right there!*

Roger! Mom says to the wall, Keep it down. The end of the world is on!

Dad says, Don't distract the man, he's making the leap, whoever he is.

How could anyone do it at a time like this, Mom says to Dad.

At a time like this, he says, how could they not?

When they do it, Mom whispers into Dad's shoulder: This is your last chance for it. Mom is always teasing, yes she is. She tells him, Hurry, the horsemen are coming.

Dad makes some Dad-joke about: They're not the only ones.

Afterward they sprawl in the dark, those strange colors burning the air. They are considering the meanings of oblivion. Considering: do it again? Time for one more? But Roger, whoever he is, is crying through the wall now, and as you know, Mom and Dad never could quite get a rhythm going when Cronkite was on.

You Can Get Wet In Cooperstown

We'd been in the car for two hours, but it wasn't 'til we crossed up into Pennsylvania that vacation really hit Mom. She stopped texting. She said, *So. We're actually doing this, huh*?

Dad said, *It's time, the boys are getting older, they can appreciate it now*, and Mom said, *Other families vacation at the shore. They tan.*

Dad said, *You can get tan in Cooperstown,* and Mom said, *You can't get wet in Cooperstown.*

You can from the rain, my brother and I said from the backseat, and Dad glared at us in the mirror because the forecast we'd seen while Mom was at yoga was supposed to be our little secret, along with our other little secret we'd been working on.

Family tradition, said Dad. *My dad took me.*

Mom said, *Your dad was a drunk*, and Dad said, *So was Babe Ruth*, and Mom said, *Point being?*

Point being, Dad said, *if it's good enough for Babe Ruth it's good enough for the Bermans.*

We said, *Wait, grandpa was a drunk?*

Mom said, *No, Mommy was only kidding*, though we were getting older and would have appreciated her not calling herself Mommy.

Dad said, *No. Not the day he took me to Cooperstown he wasn't.*

We were getting older, and we could appreciate how Mom and Dad made up. So we stayed awake in the hotel listening, but they didn't do it. Dad just fell asleep. Then we couldn't sleep because Dad was snoring.

In the morning, we finished driving to the Hall of Fame. Mom kept yawning at Dad, and Dad said, *I wasn't snoring, it was the trucks on the highway.*

Mom said, *Maybe next time don't book a hotel right on the highway*, though she knew just like we did that it was his snoring, not any trucks, that had kept us up.

My dad and I stayed at this hotel, said Dad. *Family tradition.*

Maybe it's time for some new ones, said Mom. *The shore doesn't have trucks.*

We wanted to say, *Maybe you and Dad should have made up and done it.*

Dad said, *The shore doesn't have baseball.*

Mom said, *I thought you hated these players now*, and Dad said, *Oh, you'll see.*

She did see, because when the players arrived for their induction, all the fans were screaming for autographs, and we took our signs out from under our jackets, the secret ones we'd made when Mom was at yoga. Our signs said: *Cheaters! Juicers!* We were screaming, *Keep the lying bums out!*, just like we'd practiced with Dad in the garage. Dad looked crazy with his spit flying everywhere. Security kicked us out, and it started raining. We were getting older, and we knew this was Mom's last straw.

It was nice, though, on the way home, finally getting to sit up front. I wanted to put my sneakers up on the dashboard. In the backseat, my brother was crying about mom not coming back with us. In Pennsylvania, Dad honked the horn and said, *To new traditions!* My brother said, *Wait, Babe Ruth was a drunk?*, like the poor kid really thought that back then ballplayers had been good.

Three And A Half Paths To Happiness

The day after Ricky's thirteenth birthday, a present arrived from my ex. There was no return address on the package, but it had a North Carolina postmark, and it smelled like alcohol.

"Mom, that's just your imagination," Ricky said. "Maybe Dad's stopped drinking."

Ricky was excited: yes, the gift was late, but only a day late, which meant, technically, Mark had remembered it before Ricky's actual birthday. This was the first birthday since we left Mark and moved to San Diego three years earlier that he had even sent a gift. It was difficult, after all, to mail a present from a bathtub filled with vodka. He'd have to get out of the tub and get dressed. Last year for Ricky's birthday, Mark had called, which he could do from the bath. On the phone, he had called me honey and asked for the Birthday Boy. I told him not to call me honey. I pointed out that it was May, and Ricky's birthday was in April.

"I'm not drunk, honey," Mark had pleaded, though he was, of course. His words were skipping off each other. I could hear his hand sloshing through the tub.

That was last year. Now Ricky was a teenager, even if no one had informed his little body yet, and Mark had sent a gift and a card, which I made Ricky open first. Snoopy was eating ice cream on the cover, and it read:

Hey, buster! Saw this and thought of my little man—not so little anymore, I bet. Guess what else—I'm coming to see you guys! Just have to take care of a few things here first. Til I see her, tell your mom I you-know-what her. Keep hitting those bookaroos, Dad

Ricky's knees bounced off the couch, and I could feel my heart clenching around that same wobbling hope: Maybe this time Mark was actually getting better. Maybe this time we would be a family again. I should have known better. I had been a highly controlled individual since I stopped drinking. I monitored—which meant limited, really—my eating, my sleep, my fun, and my hopes, most of all as they related to Mark—a newer version of Mark—reappearing in our lives. I reminded Ricky that his dad had promised he was coming two years before; he made it to Memphis, where the bar next to his motel was advertising 2-for-1 mojitos. What I should have done was taken Ricky by his freckled, oversized ears and yelled at him (at myself), "Abandon all hope! Your dad will always let us down!"

But when I saw how sloppily the gift was wrapped, I couldn't help myself. I pictured Mark's hands shaking, messing up the scotch tape. I remembered the way his hands shook loosely when he used to dance, like they weren't connected to the rest of him. I imagined the three of us together again, going to the zoo, imitating the hippos. Ricky's tiny pale hands were shaking, too, as he unwrapped his gift. Mark had given him a self-improvement book. *Three and a Half Paths From Adolescence to Adulthood: A Teen's Primer for Success.* On the back, was a yellow sticker, on which someone had written "75 cents."

"Well," I said. "At least he knows how old you are."

Ricky took the book to his room for the rest of the afternoon. He did not return for the *Mario Kart* game I'd bought him or the reduced-fat chocolate cake I'd baked. I had a quarter-slice and played solo. I kept crashing into penguins and spinning into brick walls. I was recalling that with Mark, even temporary sobriety was no guarantee of anything. In fact, it unleashed some inner stores of cruelty that were usually suffocated under all that liquid. I wondered if it was only the drinking—on both our parts—that got us through eight years together. I wanted another quarter-slice. I drove faster, crushing little Luigi beneath my wheels.

• • •

When I called Ricky for dinner, he didn't answer, and when I went up to get him, he was on his bed reading the book, highlighter in hand. He had Mark's and my old queen-size, and he always seemed so small on it, like a single crumb left in the middle of a plate. Above his bed hung a Cold War map showing all the nuclear target sites in California. Mark had slipped it into one of the moving boxes right before we'd left him, and Ricky spent that first winter out west asking if we could move back to Carolina. Closer to his Dad, lower threat of nuclear annihilation. I told Ricky this was what adults called a tradeoff.

After dinner, Ricky returned to his room to read, and the next morning the book accompanied him to breakfast, where he announced he couldn't eat cereal anymore.

"It's not allowed on Path #2," Ricky explained.

I played along, raising my eyebrows and asking, "Path #2?"

He held up the book. "Path #2. The Superbody Superhighway. Most cereals aren't allowed. They're basically just sugar and starch. Neither is bacon or syrup or waffles, not that you make them anyway."

"Well then thank goodness for that," I said. "What, may I ask, is allowed?"

"Eggs have the right of way. And fruit and protein smoothies. But we don't have much fruit or protein in the house, I don't think. So do you think you could make me some eggs?"

Ricky pushed his glasses up on his thin nose. They were always slipping, though I'd had them refitted several times at no small cost—his whole face had a downward slope, so that it seemed he was always jutting his chin out in defiance, though I doubted he'd ever defied anyone in his life besides me. I took a pan from the cabinet and set it on the stove. I took the Olivio and egg whites from the fridge. Ricky cleared his throat.

"Can I have the real eggs? Real eggs are actually healthy. Only people watching their cholesterol use fake eggs. Dr. Lothanger hasn't said I need to watch *my* cholesterol, has he?"

I bit my tongue and got the real eggs from the fridge. When I had the real eggs good and sizzling in the pan, I said, "I'm impressed that you're on Path #2 already, considering you only got the book yesterday. What was Path #1?"

"Brainiac Boulevard. I was already doing okay with that one, considering all my honor rolls and awards, so I qualify to skip to Path #2."

"I see. Can I ask what Path #3 is?"

"You're only supposed to focus on the one road you're driving on," Ricky told me. "You take them one at a time, at least to begin with. You need all your energy in one place. Later on, they all merge together."

"It's funny there's only half a path at the end," I said. "I wonder what it is."

"I do too," Ricky said cheerfully.

I set the eggs down in front of him. Something about eggs always made me smell bacon.

"Maybe you'd let your mom check the table of contents."

"Maybe I'll let you know when I get to it." He stacked the eggs with his fork. He had a habit of building temporary cities on his plate. Then he did this whole "I am the God of Hunger" routine.

"How will you know when you're done with this second path you're on? What's at the end of the road?"

"Well, you're not ever done with it. It's sort of a lifelong thing. But once I've gained ten pounds of muscle mass or can do 100 push-ups, I'll be ready to start #3."

"I'm sure that will be any day now," I told him.

The book lay by his orange juice, begging for a spill.

• • •

The next afternoon, I went to my weekly appointment with Dr. Lothanger, my nutritionist. In the waiting room, the receptionist smiled at me. She was also Dr. Lothanger's wife. Which job preceded which, I didn't know. But I had an idea. Her teeth gleamed as though carved from the pearly gates themselves. Probably her other parts were heaven-sent too. Probably she weighed less than Ricky. As for me, I practically had two Thanksgiving turkeys stapled to my butt. Hence the nutritionist. I'd lost ten pounds, but in truth, I hadn't only done it for me. I'd lost them for Dr. Lothanger.

He was running late, and while I waited for him in his office, I fantasized: Dr. Lothanger bending me back on the table, spreading my legs as though unfolding a secret note, and, with a gleam in his gentle old eyes, whispering, "Just relax, and let's have a look here and see what's troubling you." Then I stopped myself. I had a trick that always worked: I imagined Mrs. Lothanger in my place, her body stretched beneath her husband's on the table, her legs splayed in the air, honeyed stalks arching up to some higher power beyond the florescent lights.

Eventually, Dr. Lothanger rushed in. He was breathless, and he was not the only one. He ran his hand through his hair. He recommended I stick to steamed vegetables. I said I would try.

On the way out, Mrs. Lothanger smiled at me. I'd be smiling at everyone, too, I thought, if I looked like her. My goal, though it was not the official goal written by Dr. Lothanger in my file, was to get as skinny as his wife. I too wanted to be broken in half by his touch, swept up to the ceiling by a fan's whir, disappear behind a tree. I wanted to be diagnosed by the doctor's tongue that flicked over his thin pink lips when he studied my chart, I wanted to be groped by those hands that had held a stethoscope to so many fluttering, overworked hearts.

• • •

At home, Ricky was doing pushups in the living room. Trying to, anyway. Probably he'd started out doing pushups, but what

I found him doing didn't quite qualify. His tiny arms were bending wildly, as if they had no bones. His neck and ears were flushed red.

"Ricky, are you alright?"

He made gurgling sounds. I put my purse on the coffee table. "Honey?"

"Thirty-eight," he whispered. "Thirty-nine."

He collapsed onto the carpet and rolled over onto his back. "Water," he said.

In the kitchen, the phone rang. It was Mark, and in that rushed, overexcited tone he adopted whenever his blood alcohol level came dangerously close to zero, he told me everything: he was staying in a motel outside of Asheville, and he hadn't had a drink in two weeks, and he was on his way to come see us. When he asked if Ricky had gotten his gift, and if he liked it, he sounded astonished at himself, at what he'd been capable of, like a child who's brought home his first A on a spelling test after three years in second grade.

"I'd have Ricky tell you himself," I said, "except that he can't move his arms right now."

"You don't sound very happy," Mark said.

"It's that close attention to my feelings that made us such a great pair," I said. "The book is from 1986. I don't think the nutritional advice is even true anymore."

Mark laughed, hoarsely, and when he did, I was 25 again, back in Raleigh, throwing darts into the bar's ceiling, his scruff scratching against my neck and his liquored breath hot in my ear, telling me that when we got home, he was going to do you-know-what to my you-know-what.

"They're always coming up with something new," Mark said. "Next year, bacon will prevent heart disease. After that, it will cause spinal cancer, and organic milk will save us."

I filled a glass with water. Outside the window above the sink, our grass was growing long and yellow. "Did you get it at a yard sale?" I asked Mark.

"You always want to put a price on things."

"It *had* a price on it."

"Is it making him happy or isn't it?"

"It's not making *me* happy," I said.

"So noted. But it wasn't for you," Mark said, though I suspected that he had intended his gift to reach me exactly as it had.

For dinner, I heated up some reduced-fat macaroni and cheese. Ricky asked for eggs.

"You had eggs this morning."

He peered over his book. "And yesterday," he reminded me. "Eggs are good for you."

"They have the right of way?"

"Exactly," he said. "Do we have any vegetables you can mix in?"

I surveyed the fridge. Its shelves, haggard and low-sodium, hummed icily that I was a bad mother, deficient in vegetables and protein and men and wisdom. I shut the door on its indictments and frowned at Ricky.

"We really should have fresh vegetables," he said. "They're pretty vital to success on the Superhighway."

"Maybe you can get some when you go grocery shopping on Saturday morning."

"That's when I have chess practice," Ricky said. "Also, I can't drive."

"Exactly."

Ricky gave me his "cute" smile. One strand of hair, longer than the others, came down over his glasses. His braces were orange and green, the colors of the futuristic nation in some sci-fi book trilogy he loved. Green was for nature, he had told me, and orange for fire.

"Well, kiddo." I opened the freezer. "I could heat up this frozen casserole and then separate out the broccoli and carrots and corn and put them into some sort of omelet?"

"That's gross," he said. "But okay." He added, "Thanks, mom, I appreciate it," and right then, I would have scrambled that child 1,000 eggs, I would have never stopped, like that book I used to read him when he was little, *Strega Nona*, where the pasta overflows the pot and then the kitchen and then the house and then the entire village. That would have been us. Eggs would be bursting out the windows. I'd be sleeping on a bed of eggs. What a pair, me on a bed of eggs, and Mark across the country in a tub of gin. I laughed, which Ricky ignored, having long since chalked up my sudden laughs to the indecipherable workings of women.

After dessert—Ricky refused; I finished off his cake, bite by methodical bite—he informed me that another key to the Superhighway was making sure you were driving at the right time and getting plenty of rest.

"Rest is important," I agreed. "Especially before driving."

Once, years before, after an all-night bender in which we'd gone shot for shot with some German tourists, Mark had hit a school bus. I freaked out, but it was empty, about to begin its morning pickups. I'd snapped my collarbone, and when I went to the hospital, they told me I was pregnant, and when I went to AA, they told me I wasn't an alcoholic, I was only dependent on Mark. Also young and stupid. That was what my mom said. So terrified of the world's disorder, so scared of my own weaknesses, that I hid from them behind a man and a bottle. That was what my therapist told me. I didn't like either woman. I went through the steps, anyway, and I hadn't touched a drop since. But none of the steps ever worked for Mark, not for long.

"So I need to go to sleep by nine every night," Ricky was telling me.

"Wasn't it just last week you were begging for a later bedtime? Now you want to go to sleep even earlier?"

"Things change," Ricky said. He picked up the book and read, "That's the problem with adults. They work nine to five and sleep midnight to seven. If they slept nine to five at night, and worked five to noon, everyone would be happier and more productive."

That was probably true, I conceded. I tried to remember when I had been happiest. Probably that year after college, when I didn't work at all, and we lived and drank off the $30,000 Mark's mother left when she slipped shoveling snow. That was before the school bus.

"I'm also going to need to sleep in pitch blackness. Like, complete dark. It tricks the body into thinking it should be growing while sleeping. It will help me gain extra inches."

"I'm not sure about that. I may have to ask Dr. Lothanger."

Ricky groaned, and slapped his forehead. "Mom, you, like, love him. He'll probably tell you whatever you want to hear."

"Ricky, that's not appropriate. He's my nutritionist."

"Well, he's not *my* nutritionist. Besides, what does sleeping have to do with eating? There's science behind this. You can't argue with science."

"Maybe I'll ask Dr. Lothanger about the science of eating eggs for every meal."

"Tell him how we don't have any vegetables," Ricky said. "Tell him how your diet is actually just normal food with chemical substitutes for fat and sugar. Does he know about that? Besides, I'm putting away childish things. You should be proud."

I was, actually, and against my better judgment, I helped him hang a quilt over his window and rolled up towels to wedge under his door. After all, I believed in betterment. Wasn't that what I was aiming for, too, even if it scared me? We both had big, scary dreams. But that night, even though Ricky was the one submerged in a dark cave, I felt that he had locked me out of something secret, and that I was the one who was alone. I stood outside his door, looking at his X-Men poster, suddenly terrified of the mutants, and I listened for Ricky's comforting wheeze. I wondered what powers the mutants had. I went to the kitchen. Towers of dishes spilled out of the sink onto the counter, which was crumby again—it was perpetually crumby. I was very tired. I wanted Häagen-Dazs—I wanted Cheez-Its—I wanted Mark—new, sober Mark—I wanted Dr. Lothanger—I wanted to masturbate—I wanted a drink. I took off my socks and walked through our dark house, up and down, end to end, touching the walls and photos. With each step, I placed an urge under my heel and squashed it into the carpet, feeling them crunch beneath my weight, one after another, until they were almost gone.

• • •

Ricky was right about Dr. Lothanger. I did love him. Of course I did. How could I not? Everything about him—his tan, leathered skin, his silvered hair, his faint pink smirk, his touch on my wrist so light it was almost imagined—hinted at a lifetime of conquests. I wanted to be one of them. Once, my mom had asked Mark if he loved alcohol. We'd been at brunch, and Mark dipped his fingers into a mimosa, and smiled drunkenly, and said, *Wasn't love a sort of submission?*, which only then seemed stupid.

"Can I ask you a question," I asked Dr. Lothanger at our next appointment, once I had made it past his wife and we were secluded in his office, surrounded by BMI charts and health brochures and pictures of fruits and vegetables, Photoshopped to look delicious. "What do you think about a diet consisting primarily of eggs?"

Dr. Lothanger frowned in the direction of a food pyramid. "Why on earth would you do that?"

"I wouldn't," I said. "It's a friend."

"A friend, Janine?" He winked at me. "It's not a good idea, for a number of reasons. What's wrong with our current plan? You're making progress. Slow and steady, right? Turtle."

I saw myself as Dr. Lothanger saw me: meek and round, hidden in my shell.

"It's really not me who wants to," I said. "I know better."

Dr. Lothanger smiled sadly. I had to do something to remove that look of pity, and before I knew it, I told him: "It's my son who wants to."

Dr. Lothanger swiveled in his seat and opened my folder. "You have a son?"

"Yes," I said. "Yes. Of course. Ricky. He's thirteen. You'd love him. He's very skinny."

"Have you ever mentioned him before?"

"I'm sure I have," I told him, though I knew, of course, that I hadn't. Only I couldn't remember why I hadn't wanted him to know this in the first place. What had been the point?

"Your chart says you've never been pregnant," he said.

"Are you sure?" I asked. "Because I have been." Dr. Lothanger studied me, and I blushed. I shifted on the table. Beneath me, the wax paper crinkled. He pursed his pink lips. I thought of all his conquests: Ivy degrees, slim receptionist wives, ever-slimming patients.

"Neither you nor your son should be on an all-egg diet, nor any sort of all-anything diet."

Behind him, the scale stood ready and waiting, like a guillotine.

• • •

Within a week, Ricky had somehow—possibly via a backroad shortcut—qualified to move onto Path #3, which entailed planting flowers, writing letters to criminals and the elderly, excessive politeness to strangers, and, apparently, not eating meat.

"That seems like it should have been a sign back on the superbody road," I said from the patio. Ricky had refused a turkey burger for lunch, and now he was kneeling in our little garden, his forearms swallowed by Mark's old work gloves, gingerly setting all the worms to the side.

"It's not about nutrition," Ricky said. "It's about animal cruelty. The Feeling Freeway says having a sense of compassion is one of the keys to adulthood. Maybe you should consider working on that, Mom."

I thought: how come all the successful adults I knew had so very little?

"What about eggs?" I said.

"What about them?"

"They come from animals, don't they?"

"But you don't have to kill chickens to eat eggs. They just get pregnant, and then they have to sit and incubate or whatever and then give birth to them. So it's not that cruel."

"Kiddo," I said, "I got news for you."

He was driving on two roads at once now, and I guessed I sort of was too, riding shotgun. One night, he flexed for me, mustered everything he could to the surface of his tiny body. He looked mostly the same to me, a thin white freckly film, stretched over scrawny bones, but I thought about compassion, and I kissed him and said, "Very impressive, you studly son." Maybe he could tell I was only putting him on, because the next morning I woke to clanging in the garage, which we hadn't used in years. Still half-asleep, I thought that Mark had come back to us, and I brushed my teeth and hurried to the garage, ready for everything. Ricky had set up Mark's old bench press, which for some unfathomable reason had made the cross-country trip. Ricky had 15-lb. weights on each side of the bar, and he was grunting and wheezing. Squares of dawn came in through the garage door windows, glinting off tools hanging from the wall, wrenches, rakes and saws that we had also lugged with us when we went west, on the premise that when we sold the house and Mark moved into a studio, he would no longer have a yard to upkeep or a woman to impress with fixing. I had imagined, back then, that soon another man would be using the tools to mow my grass and stop my leaks. And yet here they hung, still untouched. Ricky rattled the bar back in place and in one motion dropped to the dirty concrete and started doing sit-ups, folding his little body up into itself over and over like some weird origami.

"Just asking," I said. "Is it possible to get arrested for speeding on any of these roads?"

• • •

But we were all moving faster than we had ever moved before. Ricky and I cut out meat; we ate vegetables together. Mark called from Knoxville, Nashville, Memphis, Little Rock—he said he was on his way. Ricky made friends with Jackson who played lacrosse. I lost three pounds. Jackson who played lacrosse started supervising Ricky's weightlifting. I lost three more. Mark hadn't had a drink in three, four, five, six weeks—he said he was on his way. I took up power walking. Ricky was doing Jackson's homework for him. *I'll believe it when I see it*, I told Mark. Mark said, *You will, honey, you will.* I didn't say, *Don't call me honey.* Jackson winked at me when I asked, *Isn't that cheating*? Ricky and I cut the grass.

Dr. Lothanger smiled and said I was looking good. His wife frowned at me. My hopes were barking, they wanted out. Ricky explained he was helping Jackson and Jackson was helping him, and since Bodybuilding was on Path #2 and Helping Others was on Path #3, it was sort of like killing two birds with one stone. I was hungry all the time. Ricky and I planted vegetables in the garden. Mark called from Oklahoma City; he was drinking Pellegrino. I fit into a blue dress from before Ricky was born and wore it to my appointment. I noticed Dr. Lothanger noticing. My hopes were bucking like crazy, and I grabbed them by the snout, told them to sit and behave. I masturbated while Dr. Lothanger was running late, and I didn't stop myself. Ricky asked a girl to a dance. Jackson was getting As and Bs. Ricky said the girl said she'd like to, but her parents wouldn't let her. I told Ricky I was proud. Dr. Lothanger's hand lingered on my shoulder. I asked Ricky if he was ready for the last half path. Mark called from Amarillo, said we would sit out on the patio at night and drink Diet Coke. Ricky said not quite, maybe soon, but his Compassion wasn't quite where it needed to be yet. I asked Dr. Lothanger did I need to undress. *To take your blood pressure?* Dr. Lothanger asked. I told Ricky I didn't think his Compassion was quite there either. Mark said he would fix the plumbing in the second bathroom. Ricky was breaking out in pimples. Dr. Lothanger glanced at my breasts. Jackson more than glanced. I was creeped out. Ricky looked taller; we measured him, almost an inch. I wasn't really creeped out at all. Ricky started wearing cutoffs. My hopes were frothing at the mouth. I heard Ricky in his room whispering, *People will respect me people will respect me people will respect me.* Mark called from Albuquerque, told me he was in the bathtub, and it was filled with water, only water. My hopes ran loose, and I didn't chase after them. I was always hungry. Ricky was always angry. An arsonist wrote Ricky that he'd inspired him to get his GED. The school wrote me that Ricky's grades were slipping. I went up to his room to have a talk about it. That was when I found the steroids.

• • •

It was our first fight as teenager and mother, and like all firsts, we stumbled through, each making our mistakes.

"You don't want me to be happy!" he screamed as I confiscated the pills.

"Of course I do. But steroids are dangerous."

"Yeah, well, so is drinking. But that never stopped you and Dad."

"Ricky, that's not appropriate. We've all made mistakes."

"Some of us more than others!"

"Hey now, Mister. What is that supposed to mean? This whole thing is getting silly, and it's not going to get you anywhere. Sorry, but it's just not. There aren't just rules you can follow to become a different person. Life's not that simple. Plus now your grades are slipping. Did you get this stuff from Jackson? What do you suppose Dr. Lothanger would say about it?"

"He'd say he hates you," Ricky screamed. "He'd say he hates you, and he thinks your little crush on him is stupid. He'd say he thinks you're ugly, and Dad would say the same thing!"

I bit my lip. "This hardly sounds like my son on the Feeling Freeway," I said.

"He'd say you're just an old mom!" he screamed, and he slammed the door on me. I tried to tell myself it was just the steroids talking. I reminded myself what he was up against: boys wearing jerseys in the hallways on game days, that sudden migration to the back of the bus.

The next day, Ricky's school called. There had been a fight. The nurse assured me the other boy was being dealt with, and I told the nurse I would come get Ricky.

On the way home, he wouldn't look at me. He held the ice pack to his eye and tapped his head against the car window. His lip was swollen. It seemed the other boy had smashed in his jaw a little, so that it wasn't jutting so much. "It's because I tried to stand up for myself," he whispered. "That's all I wanted to be able to do was stand up for myself. I can't even do that." I felt a pain beneath my stomach. I often liked to pretend that the doctors hadn't cut our cord at birth. They had only made it invisible, and endless and retractable, too, so that even when he was at school we were still connected. When he would get into trouble (not since fourth grade) or get pushed around at recess (all the time, though this was the first instance I could recall of an actual beating-up), I imagined I could feel a tug, drawing me from my own whirring little problems to him. I imagined that one day, when he was finally ready for the world, I would cut the cord, and he would go sailing away, as if without me, he'd be weightless.

• • •

That night, Mark called. I cried and screamed and told him not to come. "That book is the worst thing you've ever done."

"I'm not sure you've thought through all the things I've done," he said. "Look, I was just trying to be nice to Ricky. I'll make it up to you when I get there."

"Don't. Don't come. I don't want you to. I'm going to marry my doctor, I think."

"What doctor? You mean the Lothanger guy? He's a nutritionist, not a doctor," Mark said. "You're not really marrying him, are you?"

"Nutritionists are doctors."

"Really? Does he do surgeries? Where did he do his residency? Did he ever work a 72-hour shift? Does he save lives, Janine?"

"Yes," I said. "He does." I imagined that Dr. Lothanger was on the verge of saving mine.

"Look," Mark said. "Forget about the good doctor. I'm sober, and I love you, and I'm coming to get you. I can't promise I'll make you happy because I'm not sure anyone can make you happy. But if anyone can it's me, and I'm going to come try one more time. I owe it to you."

"Don't bother," I said. "You ruin everything you touch."

I was thinking mostly of me.

• • •

For my next appointment with Dr. Lothanger, I wore a dark brown dress with a plunging neckline. I spritzed perfume over the tops of my breasts and my neck. Ricky couldn't get what he wanted, or maybe it was still too early. But shouldn't I have a chance? In the reception room, Dr. Lothanger's wife barely looked at me.

In his office, Dr. Lothanger weighed me and listened to my heart. He was weighing many things, many options, considering whatever it was we had gotten into and sifting through treatments. Finally he looked at my chart, not at me, and he sighed.

"You have made phenomenal progress, Janine," he said. "Really, I mean that. Whatever has come over you over these last two months, I want you to keep it up. But you've reached your goal and then some. Twenty-five pounds! You certainly don't need me anymore."

I wanted to scream.

"It's always bittersweet when a patient doesn't need me anymore, because it means they're moving on, but also that I've done my job, though in this case, I can't take much credit. So on the one hand, I'm so proud of you. On the other hand, this is goodbye for us."

I tried to smile. So did he. I imagined his wife had forced him into this. He stood and stuck his hand out toward me. I'd find a note there like in the movies, informing me where we'd begin our affair. But his palm was clammy and empty. I felt only his wedding ring against my finger.

• • •

I could barely drive I was crying so much. Why hadn't I controlled myself? What had I been thinking? When I got home the house was empty and still and quiet.

"Ricky?" I called.

Then the house felt full, dangerously full, as though someone was hiding somewhere.

"Jackson?"

No answer. Then I saw there was a voicemail: it was from Mark. He sounded extremely drunk:

Honnneeeyy, I'm there, I'm ... allllmost there. I'm coming soon! Honey, I ... I ... I'm here now!! I see ... I see you!!! You, you, you look so beautifullll, you ... what? Do you know about Ricky, do you know about Ricky? Does he love me? Honnneeyyyyyyyyyy!!!!!

My breathing came quick and ragged. I understood—I knew, with perfect clarity—that Mark was here. "Honey?" I said. The house was quiet. I wanted something. I realized what I wanted was a drink. I wanted a drink so badly. I opened the fridge to see if Mark had stocked it. But it was empty. I was shaking with want. Mark was in my bedroom. He was going through my lingerie, finding the old familiars, scrunching them to his nose. He was in the tub. Or he had taken Ricky and I would never get him back. I heard a noise in the garage, a sort of scraping choke. For some reason, I thought: Mark is strangling our son, he is choking him to death to punish me. I grabbed a knife and ran out to the garage. Ricky was trapped on the bench press. Giant weights were stacked on each side of the bar, which rested on his upper chest, just beneath his neck, pinning him down.

I dropped the knife and ran to Ricky and knelt next to him, wiping his sweaty tears from his cheek. I wedged my fingertips under the bar, but I couldn't lift it. But I did what I could, I took as much weight as I could for my baby.

"You're supposed to have a spotter," he whispered. "But I don't have anybody."

"Where's your Dad?" I said.

"Dad?" Ricky said, as if that thought might give him the strength to throw the bar off. "Is Dad here?"

Yes, I wanted to say. Dad is here. But he wasn't. Of course not. I understood that now. He was nowhere close, and even if he was, it hardly mattered. Probably he was floating in a gin-filled motel bathtub somewhere between North Carolina and California. He was splashing like a child, singing the way he used to whenever the alcohol soaked in just right and gave his skin a luster that reminded me no matter what, he was the best boy I would ever love. In the back of his drunken brain, he clung to the impossible notion that he would make it back to us, that he was slowly and steadily on the road home.

Ricky asked me, "Can you lift it?" His skin was warm and red and tight. His pale little arms shook. My knees and fingers felt numb.

"I can't," I said. "I'm only an old mom."

"Maybe you can take the weights off the bar."

"Yes," I said. "Yes, of course I will."

"Thanks, Mom," he said, almost nothing left to the words after they had squeezed under the bar and through his throat. Outside, the sun was setting on us, over and over, sending comforting orange beams in through the windows across Ricky's face. His jaw quivered. His glasses were wet. His braces had caught a piece of egg, a little yellow bit that had not quite made it to its destination.

Ben Hoffman's fiction has won the *Chicago Tribune*'s Nelson Algren Award and been published by *American Short Fiction*, *Granta*, *The Missouri Review*, *Zoetrope*, and others. The recipient of a Carol Houck Smith Fellowship from the Wisconsin Institute of Creative Writing and a Wallace Stegner Fellowship from Stanford University, he now lives in Chicago.